30198
J

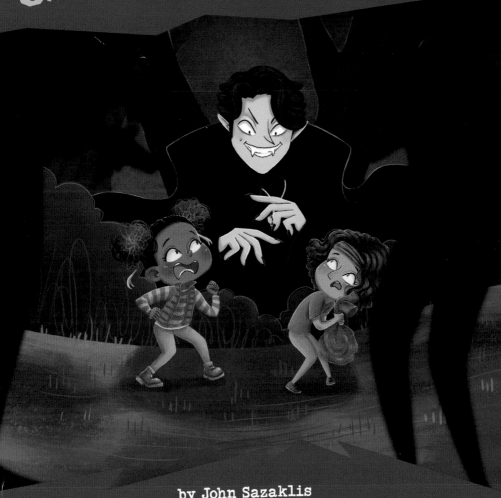

BOO BOOKS

CAMPFIRE VAMPIRE

by John Sazaklis

illustrated by Patrycja Fabicka

PICTURE WINDOW BOOKS
a capstone imprint

Boo Books is published by
Picture Window Books
A Capstone Imprint
1710 Roe Crest Drive
North Mankato, Minnesota 56003
www.capstonepub.com

Cataloging-in-Publication Data
Sazaklis, John, author.
Title: Campfire vampire / by John Sazaklis.
Description: North Mankato, Minnesota : Picture Window Books,
        [2019] | Series: Boo books | Summary: Athena, Gia, and
        their mothers are camping at the Skull Valley Campground
        making s'mores when a talking bat gets tangled in Gia's hair,
        and two pale and spooky strangers appear out of nowhere—
        but these vampires are looking for something sweeter
        than blood.
Identifiers: LCCN 2019003587| ISBN 9781515844853 (hardcover) |
        ISBN 9781515844914 (eBook)
Subjects: LCSH: Vampires—Juvenile fiction. | Camping--Juvenile fiction.
        | Horror tales. | CYAC: Horror stories. | Vampires—Fiction. |
        Camping—Fiction. | LCGFT: Horror fiction.
Classification: LCC PZ7.S27587 Cam 2019 | DDC 813.6 [E]—dc23
LC record available at https://lccn.loc.gov/2019003587

Shutterstock: ALEXEY GRIGOREV, design element, vavectors, design
element, Zaie, design element

Designer: Tim Palin and Ashlee Suker
Production Specialist: Laura Manthe

Printed in the United States of America.
PA71

TABLE OF
CONTENTS

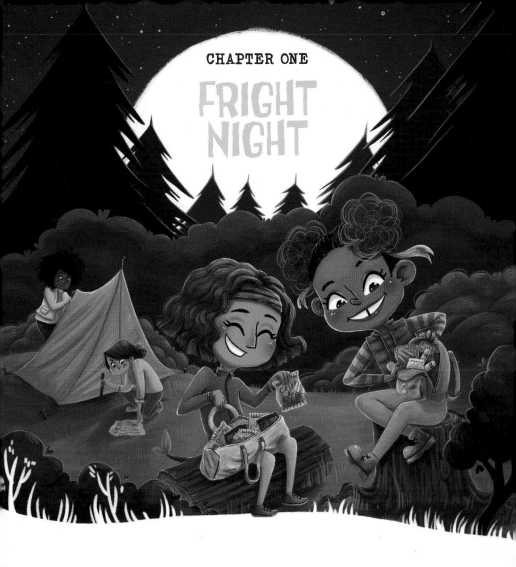

CHAPTER ONE
FRIGHT NIGHT

The sun set on Skull Valley
Campground. The forest turned
dark and cold quickly.

Athena and her best friend, Gia,
pitched their tent.

Their moms lit a roaring fire.

"Let's roast marshmallows!"

Athena suggested.

Gia excitedly agreed.

Just then, something moaned in the nearby woods.

WoOooOOOoo

Athena got scared. "What was that?" she asked.

"Probably just the wind," her mother replied.

"Maybe a ghost!" said Gia, joking. "Like in those spooky stories at the library."

The voice came again. "I want some more . . ." it moaned.

Athena jumped. "It's coming from behind that bush!" she said, pointing.

Her friend frowned. "Don't be silly," Gia said.

Gia walked over to the bush and peeked inside.

"Just as I thought," she said. "There's nothing in here."

FWIP FWIP FWIP

Suddenly a giant bat flew out and into her hair!

CHAPTER TWO

HAIR SCARE

"Ah!" Gia screamed and ran.

"I told you there was something in the woods!" Athena cried.

The bat flapped wildly in Gia's curly hair.

"I want some more . . ." it hissed through sharp fangs. "I want some more . . ."

"It wants to bite me!" Gia
screamed.

Athena bravely took off her coat.
She threw it over the creepy critter.

"Gotcha!" she shouted.

Athena scooped up the bat in her coat.

"I want some more . . ." it screeched.

"I didn't know bats could talk," Athena said.

"That's because it's not just a bat," Gia said. "It's a vampire!"

"Don't be silly," Athena said. "There's no such thing as vampires."

Suddenly a man in a black cape appeared behind them.

"AAAAAAHHHH!" screamed Gia. "It *is* a vampire!"

"You have something I want," the man said. "Give it to me, please."

The vampire reached for the girls with long white fingers.

"I told you! He wants to bite us!"
Gia shouted. "Run!"

Gia and Athena ran as fast as
they could back to the campfire.

"Mom! Mom!" Athena yelled.
"There's a vampire trying to get us!"

They were too late.

CHAPTER THREE
SPOOKY KOOKY

"Another vampire!" screamed Gia.
A pale longhaired woman
was with their mothers. Her eyes
and teeth glowed bright in the
moonlight.

"Please give me what you have,"
she said.

Suddenly the man appeared
behind them.

"There you are, little ones," he
said with a creepy smile.

His teeth looked like fangs.

"We are surrounded!" yelled Gia.

Athena was brave once more.

"I'll save us!" she yelled.

She threw the bundled-up bat

straight at the stranger. *WHUMP!*

"Bull's-eye!" cheered Gia.

The man tumbled and bumped
into the woman.

When Athena's coat fell away,
the bat was gone. In its place was a
little girl!

"Mommy! Daddy!" she cried.

Athena's mother helped the people up.

"This is Mr. and Mrs. Dracoulias," she said. "They were looking for their daughter, Lillian."

"Thank you for finding her," said Mrs. Dracoulias.

"She must have turned into a bat and flew off," Gia whispered to Athena.

Lillian looked up at them with sad eyes. "I smelled something yummy and just wanted some more," she said.

Her parents were confused. "Some more of what?" they asked.

"I know!" Athena cried. "She wants *s'mores*!"

"There's plenty for all of us,"
said Gia.

The families sat together and
made s'mores.

"Mmm," said Lillian, eating the
treat. "May I have some *more*?"

The girls laughed.

Soon it was time for Athena and Gia to go to bed.

Lillian had to leave, too.

"Nice meeting you," said Athena.

She and Gia waved goodbye to their new friend.

"I can't believe we met real vampires!" Gia said.

"What are you talking about?" asked her mom. "There's no such thing as vampires."

Suddenly there was a rustling in the trees. Athena and Gia looked up and saw three bats fly away in the moonlight.

AUTHOR

John Sazaklis is a *New York Times* bestselling author with almost 100 children's books under his utility belt! He has also illustrated Spider-Man books, created toys for *MAD* magazine, and written for the BEN 10 animated series. John lives in New York City with his superpowered wife and daughter.

ILLUSTRATOR

Patrycja Fabicka is an illustrator with a love for magic, nature, soft colors, and storytelling. Creating cute and colorful illustrations is something that warms her heart— even during cold winter nights. She hopes that her artwork will inspire children, as she was once inspired by "The Snow Queen," "Cinderella," and other fairy tales.

GLOSSARY

cape (KAPE)—a piece of clothing that hangs over the shoulders, arms, and back

creepy (KREE-pee)—something that is scary and a bit strange

critter (KRIT-uhr)—a small animal or creature

fangs (FANGZ)—long, pointed teeth

pitched (PICHT)— to put up something in place, like a tent

s'more (SMORE)—a treat made with chocolate and roasted marshmallow between graham crackers

DISCUSSION QUESTIONS

1. Do you think the Dracoulias family were vampires? Why or why not?

2. Do you think Athena and Gia will be afraid of vampires on their next camping trip? Why or why not?

3. What is your favorite illustration in this book? Explain why.

WRITING PROMPTS

1. Writing scary stories can be a lot of fun! Try writing your own scary story to share.

2. Draw a monster. Then give the monster a name and write a few sentences about it.

3. Write a story about your own camping experience. If you've never been camping, write about where you'd like to go on your first trip!

SCARED SILLY JOKES!

Where do vampires wash up?
In the bat tub.

What do you get when you cross a snowman with a vampire?
Frostbite.

Why did the vampire go to school?
To learn the alphabat!

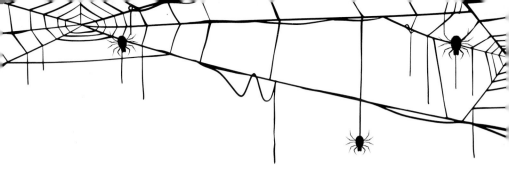

Why is baseball a vampire's favorite sport?

Because of all the bats!

Why are vampires tough to get along with?

They can be a pain in the neck.

BOO BOOKS

Discover more just-right frights!

ATTACK OF THE CUTE

CAMPFIRE VAMPIRE

THE HAUNTED BACKPACK

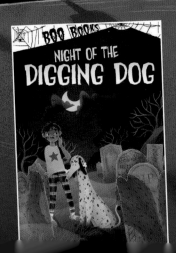

NIGHT OF THE DIGGING DOG

SCARE BALL

WITCH'S STEW